WRITTEN AND ILLUSTRATED BY BERNICE MYERS

Not THIS Bear!

NANCY PEARL PRESENTS
A BOOK CRUSH REDISCOVERY

two lions

For my loving granddaughter Olivia
—B. M.

Published by Two Lions, New York

www.apub.com

Amazon, the Amazon logo, and Two Lions are trademarks
of Amazon.com, Inc., or its affiliates.

ISBN-13: 9781477825617
ISBN-10: 1477825614

Library of Congress Control Number: 2014948124

Book design by Abby Dora Dening
The illustrations were rendered in ink and crayon.

Printed in China

Back in the 1970s, I worked as a children's librarian for the Detroit Public Library system. I spent much of my working day on the bookmobile, which at that time served areas of the city that were far from any neighborhood library. For many of the children the bookmobile served, these weekly visits were virtually their only contact with the world of books and reading outside of school.

I was a newly minted librarian, and I wanted to make sure that every child visiting the bookmobile would leave with a book that he or she would love. There were some go-tos for the middle grades: anything by Beverly Cleary, but *Beezus & Ramona* or *Henry Huggins* for sure. John D. Fitzgerald's *The Great Brain* and its sequels were another sure bet, as were *Homer Price* by Robert McCloskey and *Mr. Pudgins* by Ruth C. Carlsen. What linked these books in my mind? Their humor, of course. You couldn't read them without laughing out loud.

And when I looked for a picture book that would entertain and delight those preschoolers who came with their parents or older siblings to the bookmobile, my first choice was Bernice Myers's *Not THIS Bear!*. It's the delightful story of a little boy named Herman who has made plans to visit his aunt Gert. On his way to her house, a passing bear sees Herman and is sure that he's the Bear family's cousin Julius and invites Herman to his home for a long visit. It takes some work before Herman convinces the family that he is definitely not their cousin Julius and most definitely not a bear. When at last he succeeds, the bears all wave good-bye to him, and he starts back on his interrupted trip to Aunt Gert's house. But then . . .

This is a book to share with three and four year olds, while those beginning to read on their own will enjoy picking out words they know and learning new ones.

It's a joy to bring Bernice Myers's *Not THIS Bear!* back for a whole new generation of young readers, their parents, their teachers, and their caretakers.

—NANCY PEARL

Little Herman
went to visit his
aunt Gert.
He got off the bus
at the last stop.
But he still had
a short walk
to her house.

It was
very, very
cold.

And to keep warm,
Herman pulled himself
deeper inside his
long, FURRY coat.

And he pulled
his big, FURRY hat
down
down
over his face.

He looked just like
a BEAR–

which is funny,
because that is exactly
what a passing bear
thought he looked like.

"YOU MUST BE MY COUSIN JULIUS!"
said the bear.

Grabbing Herman by the hand,
the bear ran with him to his cave.

"LOOK WHO I FOUND AT THE EDGE OF THE WOODS!" he shouted.

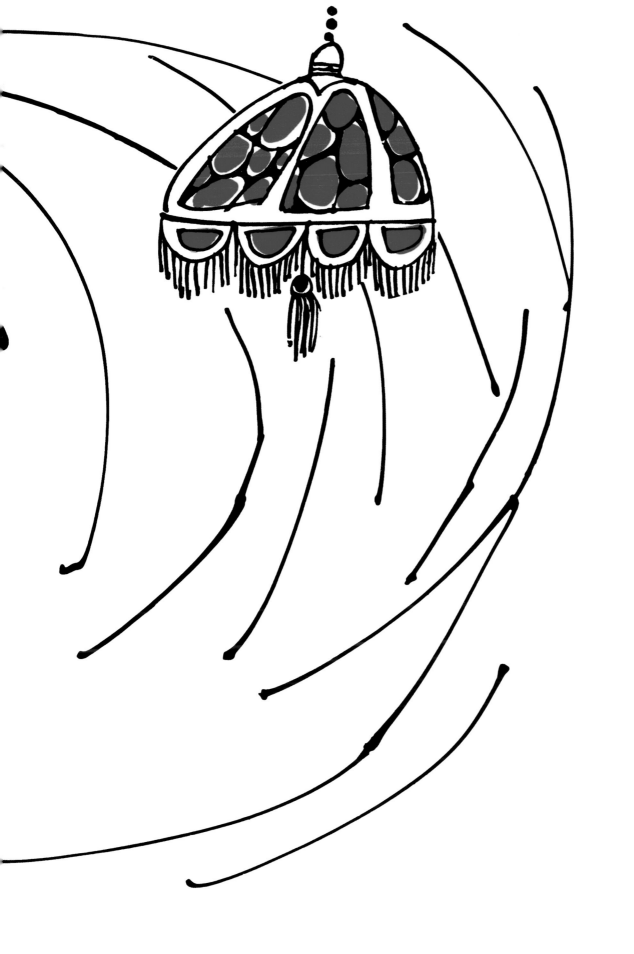

All the bears ran over and
kissed Herman hard and wet.

"COUSIN JULIUS, COUSIN JULIUS!"
they shouted.

"My name is Herman,"
said Herman.

But no one even heard.
They were so excited.

"I'm not a bear . . . ,"
Herman said.

"DINNER IS READY,"
Mama Bear called.

"TAKE YOUR PLACES.
COUSIN JULIUS, YOU SIT HERE."

When Mama Bear served the soup,
all the bears lapped it up
with their tongues.

But not Herman.
He ate politely with a spoon
that he happened to have
in his pocket.

And when the vegetables were served,
Herman ate with a fork that
he happened to have in his pocket.

The bears were amazed.
"MY, MY!" Big Brown Bear
stared at Herman.
"HOW SMART YOU ARE
TO LEARN A TRICK
LIKE THAT."

And all the bears clapped,
as if they were watching
a circus act.

Poor Herman.
He wasn't a bear.
He was a little boy.

He was sure of it.
But the bears were just
as sure that Herman
was their cousin Julius.

"So," thought Herman,
"I'll just prove
I'm really a BOY!"

 He began to SING

and DANCE

 and WHISTLE;

TIE his shoelace
and

STAND on his head—

—all the things a BOY
knows how to do.

But whatever he did, the bears still
thought Herman was a bear.
And they clapped even harder
at his tricks.

"SEE WHAT HAPPENS," said Papa,
"WHEN A BEAR HAS A CHANCE TO GO
TO THE BIG CITY AND LEARN A TRADE."

"WHAT A CLEVER COUSIN
WE HAVE," said Big Brown Bear.
And he yawned and went outside.

Big Brown Bear looked at the sky
and announced the time of year—winter.

"AFTER MAMA'S BIG MEAL
WE WON'T HAVE TO EAT AGAIN
UNTIL SPRING," he said.

And all the bears got ready to sleep.

"REMEMBER, WE SLEEP FOR
AT LEAST TWO MONTHS,"
said Big Brown Bear.

"Two months!" said Herman.
"I only sleep one night at a time.
During the day I go out and play.
I'm not sleeping through the winter!"

"BUT ALL BEARS DO,"
said a baby bear.

"Not THIS bear,"
answered Herman.
"I like winter," he said.

"HE LIKES WINTER,"
said the bears, astonished.

"Yes. I like winter.

"I like to go sledding and to skate.
I like to make snowmen and
drink hot cocoa with whipped cream.

"I like snowball fights with my friends,
and I like to make giant tracks
in the snow.

"And besides, I have to go to school."

When Herman finished speaking,
there was a long silence.

Then Big Brown Bear spoke.
"PERHAPS YOU AREN'T
A BEAR AFTER ALL.
IN FACT, NOW THAT I LOOK
CLOSER, YOU DON'T EVEN
HAVE A NOSE LIKE A BEAR."

"LOOK!" shouted a bear, removing
Herman's furry hat and coat.
"HE'S NOT A BEAR AT ALL."

And there,
shivering in the cave,
stood little Herman.

"See, I AM a boy,"
he said.

Papa Bear roared with laughter.
"THAT'S THE BEST TRICK OF ALL.
AND THE TRICK WAS ON US."

Herman put on his
furry hat and coat again.
He said good-bye to
all the bears.

"COME AND VISIT US IN SPRING."
They yawned after him.

"I will," he answered,
just to be polite.

And Herman began to walk
toward Aunt Gert's house.

He was almost out of the woods
when a big, black, burly bear
jumped out from behind a tree.

Running toward Herman,
the bear shouted,
"COUSIN BERNARD, COUSIN BERNARD . . ."

But Herman ran just as fast as
he could out of the woods.

Herman was glad when he finally
reached Aunt Gert's porch.

And Aunt Gert was very glad
to see Herman.

DISCUSSION QUESTIONS
BY NANCY PEARL

1. If YOU could draw a cover picture for this book, what would it look like?

2. Have YOU ever been mistaken for somebody else? What did it feel like?

3. What else could Herman have done to prove to the bears that he wasn't a bear? What would YOU do?

4. Luckily, when Herman was in the bear's cave eating dinner, he had a fork and a spoon in his pocket— what do YOU keep in your pocket?

5. Herman likes to do many things during the winter— what do YOU like to do?

MORE FUNNY BOOKS TO SHARE WITH PRESCHOOLERS:

Naked! by Michael Ian Black/ Debbie Ridpath Ohi.

Children Make Terrible Pets (Starring Lucille Beatrice Bear) by Peter Brown.

You Will Be My Friend! (Starring Lucille Beatrice Bear) by Peter Brown.

Strega Nona by Tomie dePaola.

Bark, George by Jules Feiffer.

Chicken Big by Keith Graves.

Rosie's Walk by Pat Hutchins.

Bubble Trouble by Margaret Mahy/Polly Dunbar.

Mouse Mess by Linnea Asplind Riley.

Unicorn Thinks He's Pretty Great by Bob Shea.